# HOW THE OLYMPICS CAME TO BE

Helen East

Illustrations by Mehrdokht Amini

First published in 2011 by The British Museum Press
A division of The British Museum Company Ltd
38 Russell Square, London WC1B 3QQ

www.britishmuseum.org

A catalogue record for this book is available from
the British Library

ISBN   978-0-7141-3144-3

Designed by Turchini Design
Printed in China by C&C Offset Printing Ltd

The papers used in this book are recyclable products made
from wood grown in well-managed forests and other
controlled sources. The manufacturing processes conform to
the environmental regulations of the country of origin.

HELEN EAST, 'a leading light in the British story-telling revival', has lived and worked all over the world, delighting audiences of every age with her endless store of stories – written, spoken, sewn and sung. Her many books for children include *The Singing Sack*, *Spirit of the Forest* and the semi-autobiographical *Dora the Storer*.

MEHRDOKHT AMINI was born in Tehran, Iran, where she studied art and graphic design. She now lives in the UK and her children's books include *El Dorado* and *The Fisherman and the Mermaid – Tales from One Thousand and One Nights*. Her work has been published in the UK, the USA, the Middle East and Poland.

FSC
www.fsc.org

MIX
Paper from
responsible sources
FSC® C008047

# CONTENTS

Family Tree of the Greek Gods   4

HOW THE OLYMPICS CAME TO BE

Day One   6

Day Two   16

Day Three   26

Day Four   34

Day Five   42

A note from the author   48
A note from the illustrator   48

# FAMILY TREE OF THE GREEK GODS

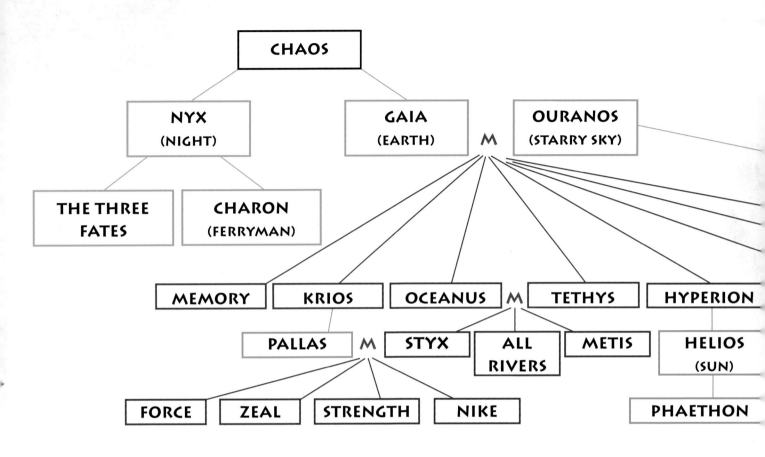

CHAOS

NYX (NIGHT)

GAIA (EARTH) M OURANOS (STARRY SKY)

THE THREE FATES

CHARON (FERRYMAN)

MEMORY

KRIOS

OCEANUS M TETHYS

HYPERION

PALLAS M

STYX

ALL RIVERS

METIS

HELIOS (SUN)

FORCE

ZEAL

STRENGTH

NIKE

PHAETHON

ZEUS

HERA

TETHYS

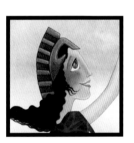

ATHENA

HERMES

ARTEMIS

APHRODITE

DEMETER

POSEIDON

ARES

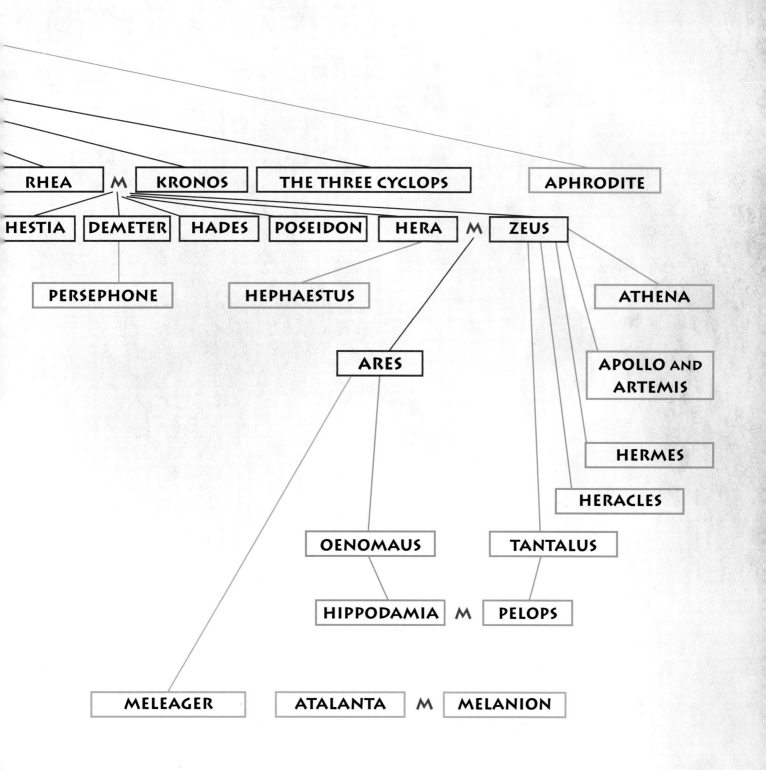

M     MARRIED
**CHILDREN FROM THAT MARRIAGE**
CHILDREN CREATED OUT OF SELF
CHILDREN (OTHER PARENT NOT MENTIONED)
LINE OF DESCENT OVER SEVERAL GENERATIONS

RHEA  M  KRONOS      THE THREE CYCLOPS      APHRODITE

HESTIA  DEMETER  HADES  POSEIDON  HERA  M  ZEUS

PERSEPHONE        HEPHAESTUS        ATHENA

ARES        APOLLO AND ARTEMIS

HERMES

HERACLES

OENOMAUS        TANTALUS

HIPPODAMIA  M  PELOPS

MELEAGER      ATALANTA  M  MELANION

**IT WAS THE FIRST DAY OF THE OLYMPIC GAMES.** Everyone who was anyone had come. Some had travelled for weeks, from all corners of ancient Greece, held safe within the Truce of Peace.

Now Olympia was packed. On every slope around the sacred grove, spectators sat, or stood if they could, at the back. A few, eagle-eyed, had even climbed the Hill of Kronos behind. They squinted through the sun down at the Bouleuterion.

In this building, far below, competitors were taking the Oath. One by one, in front of Zeus's statue, all swore on the flesh of wild boar to obey the Olympic rules. Athletes also promised they had trained for ten months, and judges declared they would be fair. Zeus was seen as the terrifying oath god, thunderbolts raised high. They knew he would strike, if any dared lie.

Finally, in one long line, the athletes stepped out in the sunshine, winding their way round the Altis grove. Past the Echo Colonnade, where the heralds and trumpeters were now noisily competing. Past the Treasuries and the Temple of Hera, to the Great Altar and Temple of Zeus.

There they stopped to prepare for sacrifices, or to pray. And to gaze in amazement at one of the Seven Wonders of the World: a statue of Zeus, the 'Shining One', in gold and ivory, thirteen dazzling metres high.

On the altars of the gods the sacred flame was flickering, ready for offerings. Liberal libations of fine sweet wine, and fat thigh meat held over slow heat, sent savoury scents high into the skies to delight the Immortals above.

The smells did rise, right to the holy heights of Mount Olympus. But most of the gods up there were far from delighted. It was already horribly hot, and the grease and smoke of burning boar made it even worse.

Only Zeus was licking his lips as he 'ate' the odour appreciatively. "Mmm," he said, "my favourite! And this one as well. Funny – they do all seem to be just for me."

Smirking, he sprawled back onto the cool stone throne in front of the long-distance 'tele-viewer', through which they could watch the events down on earth. "Look, Hera – that man there – oh no! He seems to have missed your temple too . . ."

Hera, his wife, the Heavenly Queen, gave a tight little smile. "Don't be silly Zeus, darling," she said. "You know I'm not interested in watching these earthly antics. They're nothing like proper races should be. No women for a start. Just men who can't run a thing! And such a stink – I really must get some fresh air."

The only truly refreshing breeze was blowing through the fountain room. There, as usual, was old grandmother Tethys, a little pool of watery peace around her as she sat calmly spinning. One by one the gods drifted out to join her.

"Oh Tethys!" said Hera, leaning back with a sigh against the old woman's comforting undulating bulk. "It's so hot and I'm so cross. Zeus is a gloating beast. And no one has been to my temple! It was different before wasn't it? My altar was first – I'm sure you said that! You know – in the stories you used to tell me when I was little. Remember? Go on! Tell us about the old days. When even you were young."

"Oooh" said Tethys with a great rippling laugh. "That was so long ago I can hardly remember. After all, Memory herself had only just been born!"

"Oh do tell!" said Hermes. "I love your stories too. And Hera isn't the only one who has been left out today. I thought I was supposed to be the god of athletics!"

"You?" cried Hera. "Since when –"

"Hush, my little ones," said Tethys. "I'll see what I can do. Stories eh? You'll all have to help me with the rhyme. How did it go?"

9

"*Clear streams*," they chanted.
"*Spinning dreams,*
*Spindle whirling, Silken spun,*
*So the tale is well begun.*"

"Ah yes," said Tethys. "When I was young. Well it wasn't all fun. No. Hard times the old times. My poor mother, Gaia, the Earth, she was quite worn out, giving birth to child after child. And Father, Ouranos, the Star-Studded Sky? He was no help at all. Worse in fact, because if he didn't like the look of a child he'd pick it up and push it back! You can imagine how Mother complained about that!

Especially the poor Cyclops triplets, all with only one eye. Huge they were – fought like anything to stay out.

Kronos, our little brother, was Mother's favourite. I suppose he took everything she said a bit too much to heart. So – you know what he did, don't you? Crept up behind Ouranos with the silver sickle and Slash! Oh dear. That was the end of him.

Apart from one slice that slipped into the sea below and turned to the foam that formed Aphrodite, our gorgeous goddess of love. And two splashes of gore that became the Meliae, nymphs of the ash trees. And of course the three drops of blood that fell on the earth. The Furies sprung up from those. Nasty bits of work they were. Three clawed, snake-haired goddesses of vengeance, dripping with blood. They drove poor Kronos mad in the end. No sleep, just their endless shrieks: 'As you did to your father, so will be done to you.'

Not that I think it was any excuse for what he did then. Swallowed his own children, as soon as they were born. Hera, Hestia, Demeter, Hades and Poseidon – all of them gone in a gulp.

Poor Rhea, his wife – my little sister. She begged me to help, and what else could I do? I'd always looked after her, and I was nursing her at the time, so when the last baby – the little Shining One, Zeus – was born, I quickly snatched him up and pushed him under the bed. Then, grabbing the great stone doorstop, I wrapped it in swaddling bands. As Kronos came hurrying in, bleary-eyed from lack of sleep, I waved it at him, and then popped it into his mouth. 'Congratulations,' I said, 'another son.' So that was how Zeus was saved. Then the Meliae nymphs looked after him down on earth until he was old enough to rescue you all, and fulfil the prophecy. The rest is history."

"History?" said Hera. "I'm fed up of his-story. Zeus! It's all been about *him* today. Offerings, and everything. It wasn't always like that was it?"

"Offerings?" Tethys gurgled with laughter. "Certainly not! Unless you count the special soup that Zeus offered his father when he returned from earth. He was disguised, of course, so Kronos didn't know it was him. I don't suppose he realized there was magic potion in the soup either, it smelt much too good. That was my daughter Metis's doing – very good with herbs she is. Anyway, Kronos always was too greedy for his own good. He grabbed the pot and gobbled the lot. Then promptly threw it all up again, along with everything else in his belly. Which included you children, now nicely grown up and ready to join forces in defeating your father."

"So!" said Hera triumphantly. "Zeus didn't do it on his own, did he? He needed us all to help."

"Of course he did, darling," said Tethys. "But Zeus was always the ringleader. And wily too. It takes more than force to win battles. That's why he made friends with whoever he could. He even unearthed the three Cyclops. And they were so grateful they gave him the thunderbolts and lightning that have made him the Lord of the Skies.

That's how he managed to knock out Kronos in the end. One strike threw him down to earth, another pushed him under that hill you can see down there. It's been called the Hill of Kronos ever since. Zeus even marked the spot with a thunderbolt. The first Olympic contest, I suppose you could call it. But whether that was the beginning of the Games or not –"

"No!" said Hera. "Zeus using thunderbolts was unfair!"

"Does fairness matter?" asked Tethys.

"Yes! It's in the Olympic oath the Mortals have to swear."

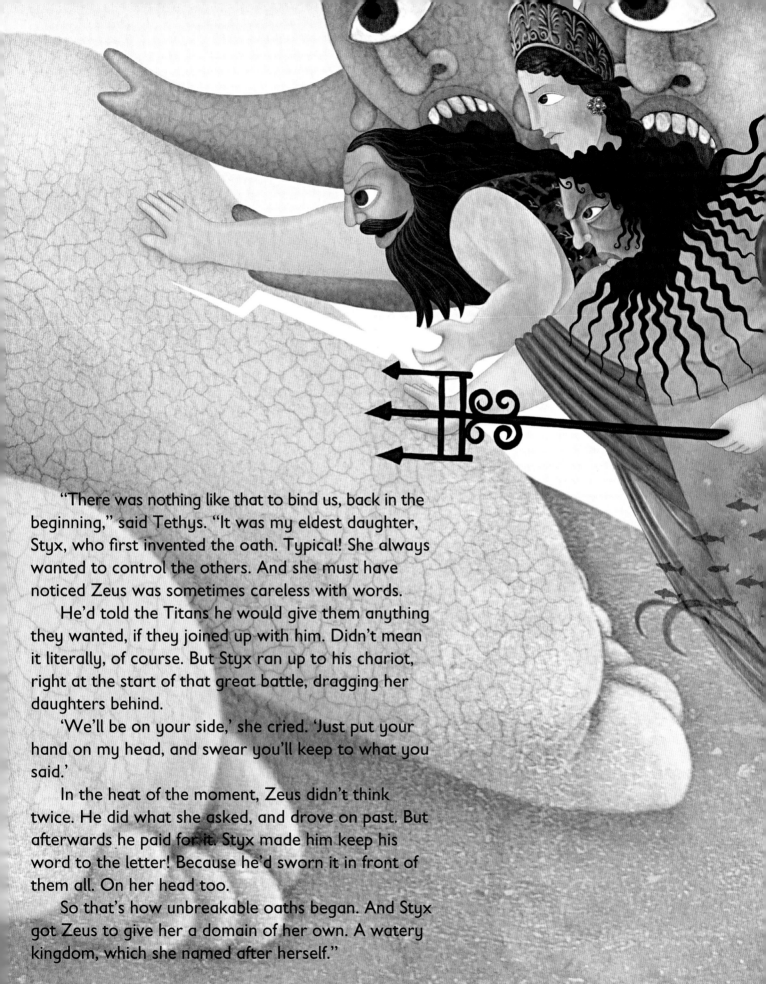

"There was nothing like that to bind us, back in the beginning," said Tethys. "It was my eldest daughter, Styx, who first invented the oath. Typical! She always wanted to control the others. And she must have noticed Zeus was sometimes careless with words.

He'd told the Titans he would give them anything they wanted, if they joined up with him. Didn't mean it literally, of course. But Styx ran up to his chariot, right at the start of that great battle, dragging her daughters behind.

'We'll be on your side,' she cried. 'Just put your hand on my head, and swear you'll keep to what you said.'

In the heat of the moment, Zeus didn't think twice. He did what she asked, and drove on past. But afterwards he paid for it. Styx made him keep his word to the letter! Because he'd sworn it in front of them all. On her head too.

So that's how unbreakable oaths began. And Styx got Zeus to give her a domain of her own. A watery kingdom, which she named after herself."

The Styx. Between the living and the dead. A great palace in the underworld, formed from a ten-channel river. Deep, dark, deadly. To pass over you must pay. A coin for Charon the ferryman. But only one way. Because there is no going back. Unless you swim. And that's impossible.

An oath, especially if it's sworn on Styx, is the same. No going back on it. Try, and you'll find yourself in deadly deep water. Mortals will be frozen to the bone. But it's worse for gods. It takes away our immortality. Harder still, perhaps, we lose our tongues too. No more stories. Nothing. That's how even Zeus was bound.

Dangerous thing to do, swear oaths. That's what they did on earth today? I wouldn't worry about missing out on that, Hera, if I were you."

"No, granny," said Hera in a very small voice. "But I don't think they were real Styx oaths. The Mortals were just promising to abide by the rules."

"Rules? Huh!" The old woman snorted with such force she snapped the thread she was spinning. "Silly fools! There never were rules in the beginning! Not when a chariot ride was a ride for life, when the first charioteer took up the reins. She was the best of all . . ." Tethys sighed, closing her eyes as if she was looking inwards.

"Don't stop!" cried Hera. "Please! She? The first charioteer? Who do you mean?"

"No more tales today," said Tethys. "It's too hot, and look – I've lost my thread. Maybe tomorrow, when the races are run and done, I might remember more."

## DAY TWO OF THE OLYMPIC GAMES DAWNED CLEAR AND BRIGHT. NOW THE REAL RACES BEGAN.

The first was top of everybody's list. The most exciting. Most dangerous. The four-horse chariot contest.

Every man, every youth, every boy – and any female young enough to be allowed – forgot all else in the struggle for spectator space above the hippodrome. Pent up within the stalls of the great ship-like starting apparatus, the horses were champing at the bit, the charioteers standing tall and proud. Then the longed-for trumpet sounded, the bronze eagle soared, the ropes dropped and they were off.

One great wave of pounding hooves, whirling wheels, cracking whips. All the watchers held their breath at the approach to the first turn, with that white stone, the infamous 'Horse Scarer'. The chariots

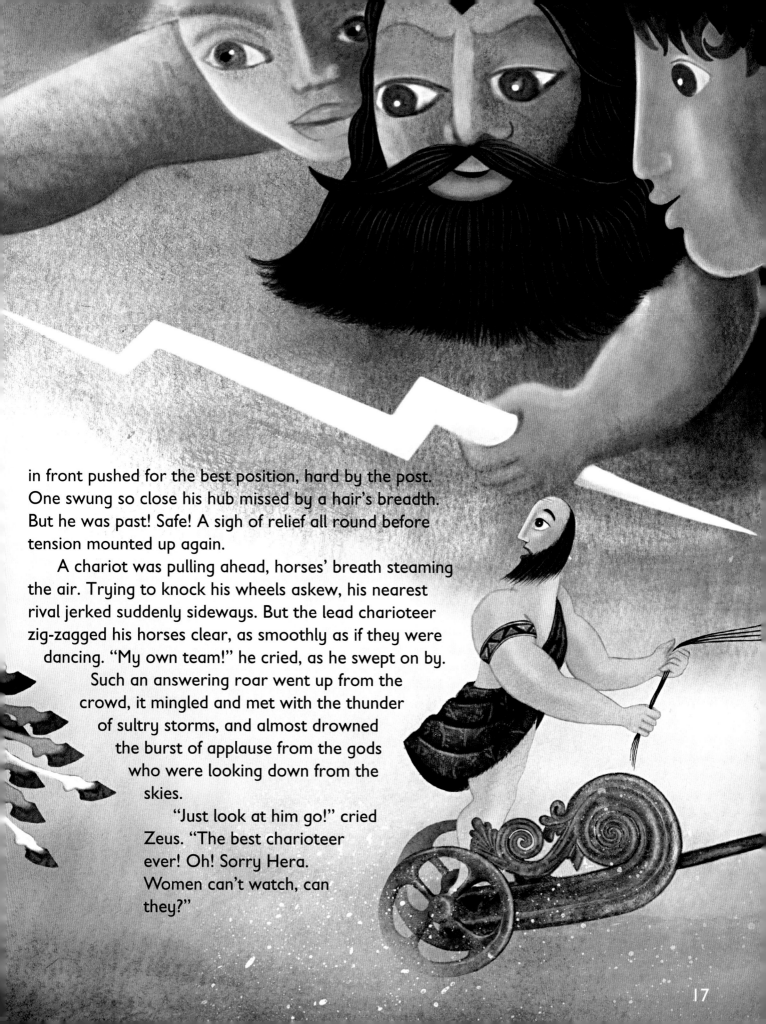

in front pushed for the best position, hard by the post. One swung so close his hub missed by a hair's breadth. But he was past! Safe! A sigh of relief all round before tension mounted up again.

A chariot was pulling ahead, horses' breath steaming the air. Trying to knock his wheels askew, his nearest rival jerked suddenly sideways. But the lead charioteer zig-zagged his horses clear, as smoothly as if they were dancing. "My own team!" he cried, as he swept on by. Such an answering roar went up from the crowd, it mingled and met with the thunder of sultry storms, and almost drowned the burst of applause from the gods who were looking down from the skies.

"Just look at him go!" cried Zeus. "The best charioteer ever! Oh! Sorry Hera. Women can't watch, can they?"

There was a gurgle from behind. "Best ever?" murmured Tethys, winking at Hera. "You have a short memory, Zeus."

"Oh yes!" said Hera, suddenly cheering up. "That story! The first charioteer. Tell us, Granny!"

"No," said Zeus, "I don't think —"

"Quite," said Tethys. "Sometimes you don't." And twirling her spindle up into the air, she sent a river of story swirling in all directions.

"You remember Styx bringing her daughters into battle, don't you Zeus? Four fine girls, all more useful than her. The eldest three — Force, Zeal and Strength — were tremendous. But the youngest was best of all. Little Nike of the white ankles. Slim as a wand, yet unyielding as iron. She leapt up behind Zeus, into the chariot, crying out in her high clear voice. 'Give me the reins, cousin, let me be your charioteer.'

You laughed, didn't you Zeus, as you tossed them to her. But no whip. No need of that for your horses that day. And it was only then, as Nike took her stance, that she looked down and saw what manner of beasts they were. The Horses of the Sun. Sparks striking from their hooves, flames tangling with their manes, smoke snorting from their nostrils.

Poor girl. She must have thought at that moment of another of her cousins. Phaethon. The unlucky one. Sweet-faced child of the Sun. When Phaethon found out who his true father was, he sought him out and demanded he prove his love. And Helios the Sun, overwhelmed with foolish fatherly pride, swore on the Styx to give him whatever he desired. Obviously he didn't know much about children — they never want what is good for them. As Phaethon proved when he insisted he wished to drive the chariot of the Sun.

You know what happened to him, don't you? Nike certainly did. She must have seen in her mind's eye the look on that boy's face, fear frozen like a mask. For as he took those same reins into his hands all was sudden chaos. Horses tearing free of grip, chariot swinging out of course. Sun's scorching breath on earth and Phaethon plunging to his death.

Nike remembered. But she didn't let it show. Calmly she took control, and those horses knew. Zeus too.

Like a knife honed by water to its keenest blade, she sliced so easily through the battlefield that day. Foe fell to left and right, fled on either side, broken and beaten behind. No doubt at all, it was her who drove Zeus to victory. Little Nike. That's what her name means of course: Victory.

Now you know why athletes down on the earth carry little statues of her. Holding victory, they hope! If they can't afford them, they simply wear her name. No best better than her."

"Nike doesn't count," said a cold hard voice. "Driving for battle isn't racing. Not strictly sport at all." It was Ares, god of war.

"Don't be awkward!" Hera scowled at her son. "You weren't even born! Tethys was there. Surely she's right?"

"Different rules." Ares looked smug. "I should know."

"What?" Poseidon sat up so suddenly he startled the starfish asleep in his beard. "Is that *you* Ares, pretending to care about rules? What about your son Oenomaus and his deadly chariot races? Killing anyone who wanted to marry his daughter!"

Ares's armour clanked uncomfortably. "Hippodamia? That girl was trouble. I admit he was a bit too careful of her —"

"Careful?" cried Poseidon. "Cruel, I'd call it. Oenomaus knew he couldn't lose. Not with the horses you'd given him. Creatures made of the wild wind! What earthly beasts could beat that? I interfered only to be fair on Pelops —"

"Pelops? *You* helped that murderous cheat?" Ares was on his feet, reaching for his dagger.

"Boys!" cried Tethys. "It's truce time! Stop winding each other up — you're tangling the tale. Now I must unknot it. *Spin back to start again. End unwound we can begin.*

Just like it happened to Pelops. Extraordinary boy. Born survivor. Maybe he was half immortal. Wasn't his father one of your sons, Zeus? That awful King Tantalus."

Hera sniffed loudly, but Tethys just grinned. "Full of himself, he was!" she said. "Must have got that from someone! Always trying to outdo everybody. Even us gods! One night he swore he could give a finer feast than any banquet we'd had up above. As he'd insisted that every god on Olympus came, of course he ran out of food.

But, being Tantalus, he wouldn't accept defeat. In a moment of madness he went to the kitchen, called his son, Pelops, and popped him into the pot. We didn't know, but being gods, we sensed something was wrong. So we left the dish untouched."

"Except for me," said a quiet voice. It was Demeter, looking very sick. "Even now I can hardly bear to think of it," she whispered. "But I had just lost Persephone, my daughter. I didn't know if I would ever see her again. I was too upset to care what I touched, smelt, or even ate. So I never noticed what was in my mouth, until I'd cracked the bone and picked it clean. Then I looked down as I put it on my plate. Oh! It was a child's shoulder blade. The left one. Given to me as food."

"Yes," said Tethys. "An unforgivable thing to do. Tantalus is forever punished for it — endlessly tantalized by food and drink he cannot reach. But it changed things for us all, even the gods. No longer do we dare to swallow mortal food.

Only Pelops came off lightly. For when Zeus too began to plead, the three Fates agreed to undo what was done. Gathering the boy together, bones, bits and all, they put him back in the cauldron and boiled it upside down. All the while they spun the thread and said the words of destiny backwards. It was extraordinary to see. The web of happening unravelled, the boy returned to wholeness."

"Except his shoulder," said Hera. "What has been chewed cannot be renewed."

"True," said Tethys. "But luckily, Hephaestus forged him a better one. A silver shoulder blade that made his left arm twice as strong. Perfect for a charioteer!"

"Just right to race Oenomaus" cried Poseidon, "and win his beautiful daughter!"

"Although he must have been a bit daunted," said Tethys, "when he rode through the palace gates and saw the twelve heads of previous suitors nailed up above.

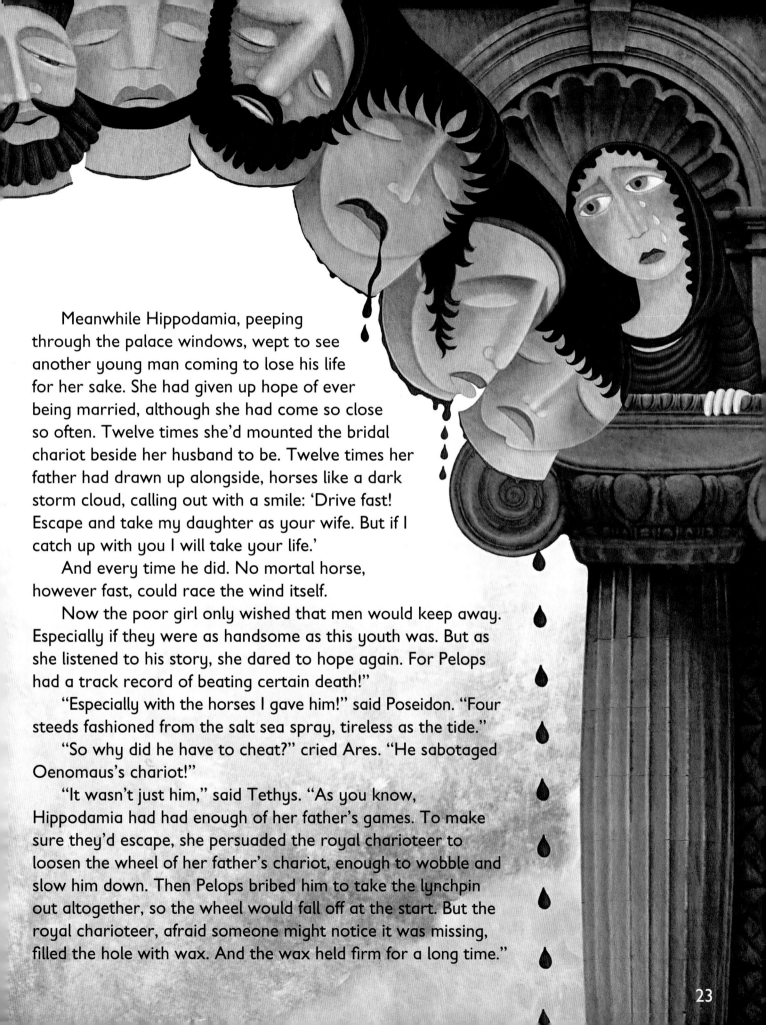

Meanwhile Hippodamia, peeping through the palace windows, wept to see another young man coming to lose his life for her sake. She had given up hope of ever being married, although she had come so close so often. Twelve times she'd mounted the bridal chariot beside her husband to be. Twelve times her father had drawn up alongside, horses like a dark storm cloud, calling out with a smile: 'Drive fast! Escape and take my daughter as your wife. But if I catch up with you I will take your life.'

And every time he did. No mortal horse, however fast, could race the wind itself.

Now the poor girl only wished that men would keep away. Especially if they were as handsome as this youth was. But as she listened to his story, she dared to hope again. For Pelops had a track record of beating certain death!"

"Especially with the horses I gave him!" said Poseidon. "Four steeds fashioned from the salt sea spray, tireless as the tide."

"So why did he have to cheat?" cried Ares. "He sabotaged Oenomaus's chariot!"

"It wasn't just him," said Tethys. "As you know, Hippodamia had had enough of her father's games. To make sure they'd escape, she persuaded the royal charioteer to loosen the wheel of her father's chariot, enough to wobble and slow him down. Then Pelops bribed him to take the lynchpin out altogether, so the wheel would fall off at the start. But the royal charioteer, afraid someone might notice it was missing, filled the hole with wax. And the wax held firm for a long time."

23

"It must have been a glorious spectacle at first. Two royal competitors, immortal blood in both their veins. A beautiful bride, bedecked in jewels, bright with joy. Two regal chariots, gleaming with gold, drawn by the horses of sea and sky. An elemental contest so swift it blurred all sight, spectators barely drawing breath to shout.

Until the very speed took its dread toll, heating the wax so it poured down. The wheel unwound and Oenomaus was flung to the ground.

He died on the spot. Down there – look. Where the 'Horse Scarer' stands, like a white ghost pointing an accusing hand.

So that day, joy met sorrow, marriage and funeral rites mingled into one. But after, Pelops gave great thanks to Zeus for victory. And that, most Mortals say, is how these Games began, and why tonight all athletes honour Pelops."

"But it wasn't just him," said Hera. "It was Hippodamia as well. She and her women held races too!"

"Yes," said Tethys, "the Heraea – dedicated to you." Hera smirked at her husband. "Tell us more about them, nanny, please!"

"No," said Tethys. "Enough for now, or I'll be tired out. Have you forgotten Selena the Moon will be full tonight? No use trying to sleep with the sky so bright. Oceanus, my dear husband, will be tossing and turning, but I, old though I am, will be up and dancing, like the revellers down below. And you, Queen Hera, should forget your cares and join us too. Even foolish Mortals know dancing is good for you!"

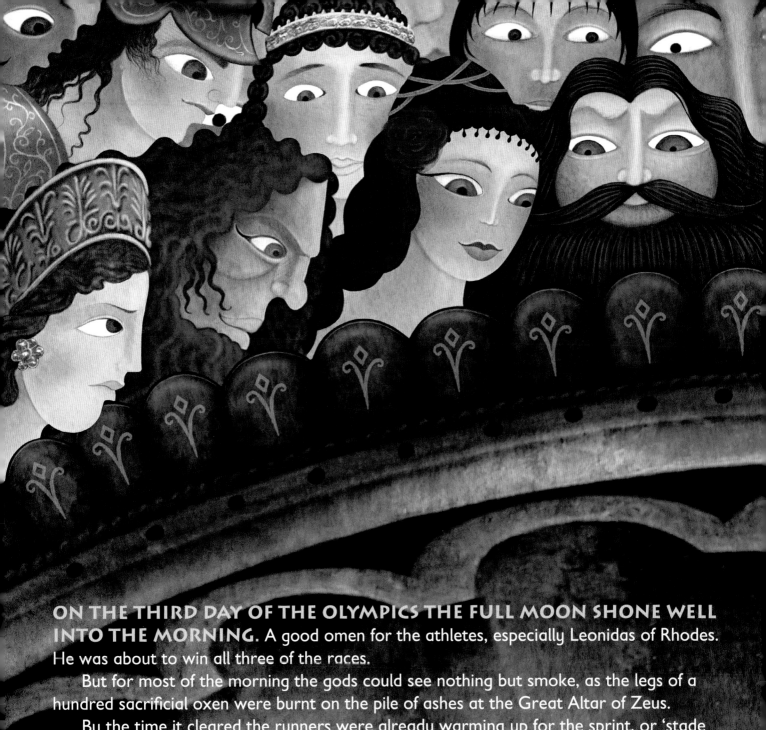

**ON THE THIRD DAY OF THE OLYMPICS THE FULL MOON SHONE WELL INTO THE MORNING.** A good omen for the athletes, especially Leonidas of Rhodes. He was about to win all three of the races.

But for most of the morning the gods could see nothing but smoke, as the legs of a hundred sacrificial oxen were burnt on the pile of ashes at the Great Altar of Zeus.

By the time it cleared the runners were already warming up for the sprint, or 'stade race'. This was the most popular of all running events. The lucky winner would be remembered by everyone, for they would give their name to the Olympic Games of that year. Many would have statues made of them too, so hundreds of years later they could still be recognized.

Like the spectators below, the Immortals were jostling to see the action, this time through the tele-viewer by Zeus's throne. Even Tethys had come, leaving the calm of her fountain house. Close behind – to everyone's astonishment – were the shadowy Fates, drawn by her tales, and stirring memories.

To Hera's annoyance, Aphrodite, the goddess of love, was settled right at the front, half perched on Zeus's knee.

"Ooh!" she cried, gazing with delight into the screen. "Isn't it clever – you can see everything! Look at that one poised to take off. So beautifully oiled and gleaming, sweat beads like jewels on his brown back!"

"He's got funny feet," said Hera. "Toes all bent."

"That's through gripping the starting sill," said Zeus. "Don't you know anything? If he pushes off too early he'll be flogged. Even if he is the world-famous Leonidas."

"Is that who he is?" sighed Aphrodite. "Well he's certainly in good shape."

"No wonder, the way he dances," said Tethys. "I could hardly keep up with him last night."

"WHAT?" The gods gaped at their old nurse.

"It looked such fun, I just joined in. Not as a woman. I know the rules. I went as a young girl. I can still feel the spring in my step."

"That's what you need for running," said Hera with a sniff. "Not toes curled like a bird! Just natural speed – like Atalanta had. She'd have beaten any of those men down there."

Artemis, goddess of the hunt, sat polishing bows and pretending she wasn't listening. But at the mention of Atalanta she looked up, smiling. "What a girl," she said. "Indomitable!"

"Rather odd, if you ask me," said Aphrodite. "More like a boy."

"We didn't ask –" began Artemis.

"Girls! Please! There are two sides to every story," said Tethys. "Maybe more, in this one. Shall I tell it?"

"But listen!" cried Zeus. "The stade race is starting!"

Far below they heard the call. "*APITE!*" GO!

"There's your answer," said the Fates. "Go on! Spin the tale. Shall we help?"

"No!" cried Hera. "You might mix up spindles!"

"Not if I use my wheel!" said Tethys. "Clever Hephaestus made it. Watch!

*Kick the wheel to make it spin,*
*Then the tale can well begin . . .*"

And before Zeus could protest again, his tele-viewer had misted up with overwhelming images of story.

"The Queen of Calydon had a son, Meleager. She left him sleeping in his cradle, warm by the fire. But suddenly she heard him gurgling, and strange voices answering. Three ancient women, all in white, were leaning over him.

The first twirled a spindle with the speed of light. 'I spin the thread of life!' she cried. 'This one has started strong.'

'I'll measure it,' the second said. 'See if the life is long.'

'No! For I must cut,' the third one sighed. She lifted a pair of shining shears, opening them wide. 'This little life will only last the time it takes that log to burn upon the hearth.'

In an instant the queen had pushed past. Snatching up the burning wood, she threw it into a bowl of water. A hiss, a twist of smoke, and the fire was out.

'I have defeated fate,' she said. 'Cheated death. I'll keep this charred log safe. Meleager can live for ever if I wish!'

Meanwhile, in the kingdom of Arcadia, Prince Melanion was born. This time the Fates agreed the boy might suffer from 'forgetfulness'. To prevent this, poor Melanion had to study day and night, strengthening his memory and sharpening his mind.

All this time, King Iasos was waiting for a son. Expecting one. Instead he got a daughter, Atalanta. He was so angry, he didn't care what the Fates said. He had the baby dumped on a hot mountain top."

"But Atalanta didn't die. She thumped her little fist against the ground so hard, a spring burst out, and kept her cool.

Artemis happened to be hunting nearby. Feeling thirsty, she followed the sound of water."

"And there she was!" cried Artemis. "A beautiful baby. Giggling to herself, quite unafraid. I brought my she-bear to suckle her.

Later I made sure a good hunter found her. He raised her as his child, teaching her all he knew. And I blessed her with the sharpest of eyes so she always aimed true, the keenest sense of smell to follow any trail. Best of all, the swiftest feet, to outrun every deer.

What a woman she became! Equal to any man. And no girlish nonsense. Until she went to Calydon, and Aphrodite started meddling!"

The goddess of love gave a golden giggle. "You can't blame me for every natural impulse," she said. "But it was a match made in heaven!"

"What? With Meleager?" Artemis was outraged. "Have you forgotten how his father failed to honour the gods? I had to send that boar to Calydon to punish him!"

"You can't blame a son for his father's faults," said Tethys. "And you might have guessed the Calydonian Boar would draw Atalanta, as well as Meleager. It was the best of beasts to hunt — and they were the greatest hunters. A perfect partnership. Except Meleager's uncles didn't want a woman in the hunting party."

"Ridiculous!" snapped Artemis. "The boar was making mincemeat of them! Only Atalanta's arrow stopped it in its tracks."

"Yes," said Tethys. "That's why Meleager gave her the tusks and skin. His uncles, however, objected violently. It turned into a terrible fight, and they were killed.

Poor Queen of Calydon. Her brothers dead, and her son blamed. Crazy with grief, she locked herself in her room. There, in the cradle, was that charred piece of wood. Kept safe for all these years. She threw it into the fire – then reached to take it back. But it exploded into white hot flames.

Atalanta, returning with Meleager, felt his hand grow hot. His skin blistered, hair blazed. In an instant he was ash.

She thought it was a punishment from Zeus. A thunderbolt. And all her fault. Her love had helped cause Meleager's death. Atalanta swore she would never love again."

"A Styx oath?" asked Hera.

"No" said Tethys. "Luckily." She smiled at the Fates. "Somehow, Atalanta's father discovered her, and brought her home. Then he insisted that she marry someone. Atalanta would only agree if he found a suitor who would race with her. 'If he can win,' she said, 'I'll marry him.'"

"Impossible!" said Hera. "No one ran as fast as her!"

"Exactly," said Tethys. "And she set rules for King Oenomaus: 'If the man loses, he will die.' She hoped no one would try. Unfortunately hundreds did – and none of them survived. No one stood a chance."

"Until Melanion came along. A friend had asked him to come as a judge, because he was famously wise. But really he came to persuade that friend not to risk losing his life.

'No woman is worth that price!' he cried.

'I agree' said a voice from behind.

Melanion turned. There was Atalanta. Eyes met. Hearts began to race.

Atalanta forgot her oath. Melanion forgot all sense.

'I've changed my mind,' he sighed.

'Don't try to win me,' she begged. 'You'll die.'

'What use is life,' he said, 'without you as my wife?'"

"But he still had *some* sense," said Aphrodite, "because he asked me for help. A most presentable young man. And of course I'll always aid anyone in love. You remember that golden apple – don't you, Hera? Athena will too, I'm sure. The prize for the loveliest goddess? And Paris chose me, didn't he, out of us three." She smirked triumphantly. "Golden apples! They're so desirable aren't they? Any real woman would do anything to win one, wouldn't they? So I sent three to Melanion, and whispered in his ear: 'As you race let each one drop when you most need your love to stop.'"

"I might have guessed it was you!" snapped Artemis. "I saw the start of the race but there was such a crowd, I missed the end. I thought Atalanta was off form. Unusually nervous."

"She was," said Tethys. "Standing alone, all eyes on her. She turned her back on everyone. Looked ahead. Concentrated on one point. The finishing post. That was all she ever saw in a contest. She felt the earth beneath her feet, and made herself forget all else.

Melanion also tried to think of nothing but the race. He held the apples hidden, took a deep breath –

'APITE!' And he was off, running for his life. But she was gaining. Like a hare, long-legged, leaping past. An apple glinted in the air, hung for a moment there, catching light like a mirror, reflecting back – a face. Atalanta stopped, shocked, to catch it and look close. Meleager, her lost love, smiled. Then he was gone. And looking up she saw Melanion, running on.

He was past the halfway point when he heard the crowd cry out. He dropped the second apple as she came up on the right. She glanced as she passed, then stopped dead in her tracks. The face in the apple this time was her own. Not as she was now, but as she might become. A bitter old woman, unhappily alone.

Melanion was metres from the finishing post. The crowd was ecstatic, but Atalanta was close. And he was tiring, slowing down. He took the third apple and turning around, handed it to her, a golden gift. Then watched as she stopped and looked deep into it. Reflected in the apple, she saw Melanion's head. As it would be if he lost the race. Cold and dead. Atalanta gave a sob, and let the apple drop. Then picked it up and, kissing it, she held it to her heart. And stood there still until she heard the winner's name called out."

"So Atalanta *let* herself lose!" exclaimed Artemis.

"Yes," replied Hera. "But she also won, didn't she?"

"Well said, Hera," smiled Zeus, to her surprise. For a moment there were loving looks between husband and wife. Then Aphrodite broke the spell.

"The tele-viewer's dark," she said. "Is it all finished down there?"

"Oh no!" said Zeus. "I didn't see who won."

Tethys glanced at the Fates, who nodded. "It was Leonidas of course," she said. "And if you want to see him do it, Zeus, watch the next Olympics. He's going to do it again!"

## IT WAS MIDDAY ON THE FOURTH DAY OF THE OLYMPICS.

Zeus was in an excellent mood. He'd made up for his disappointment the day before by spending the morning watching the wrestling below, and commentating loudly on the antics of the Italian champion, Milo of Croton, who had just won for the fifth time.

"Look what he's doing now!" he cried. "That's a real Heraclean lift!"

Hera sniffed and stalked away, but Hermes glanced at the tele-viewer and burst out laughing. Milo the wrestler was half-hidden by an enormous cow, which he was carrying over his shoulder as if it was a baby. "Just a snack for supper," he told onlookers, who cheered but kept a safe distance. The cow was kicking wildly, and its hooves were hard and sharp.

"Makes you realize why King Eurystheus was worried when Heracles threw him the Cretan bull! That was three times the size!"

"Now there's a tale for you Tethys!" said Zeus. "The lad and his labours! What about it, Hera my dear? You love stories so!"

"Well," said Tethys, smiling too. "It certainly fits with this afternoon. Boxing and then pankration – the all-strength fighting. Most of that did come from Heracles! Why, I remember when he was only a baby –"

"– the less said about THAT the better!" snapped Hera. "Heracl – no! I don't even want to hear his name!"

"Now, now," said Zeus. "You can't blame the son for his father's faults."

"Who says?"

"Tethys did," replied Zeus smugly. "Yesterday."

"So you were listening," said Tethys. "And it's true. But you can blame the father. You were certainly at fault – cheating Hera. And Heracles's mother – changing yourself to look just like her husband. That was a shameful thing to do!"

Zeus blushed and hung his head. Hera looked triumphant.

"But," Tethys smiled, "take credit when it's due, Hera. It wasn't Zeus who made Heracles a hero – it was you. If you hadn't been so hard on him, he would never have been pushed to prove himself."

"Like metal," said Hephaestus. "Put in the heat to burn the rubbish, leaving pure strength."

"Oh!" said Hera, looking surprised. "But –"

"– you knew that," nodded Tethys. "Anyway, who can even say his name without thinking first of you? Born Alcides he became Heracles. Renamed after the incident with the serpents – remember?"

"He was only a baby then, cradled in his stepfather's war shield . . ."

"Doesn't he look small!" whispered Hermes, suddenly seeing the scene spinning by. He hadn't even noticed Tethys whisking her new wheel into action.

"Don't the snakes look big," said Tethys, "slipping from Hera's basket; winding their way silently until they are close enough to strike. One hissed then, and the baby woke. Chuckling he reached to grab, and caught one in each little fist, tight about the throat. They turned, they squirmed, but he held firm, laughing at this new-found game. By the time his nurse came, both were dead, dangling limply like two soft teething toys."

"That's a proper choke-hold!" announced Zeus, watching proudly.

"And only the beginning!" laughed Tethys. "Remember what he did when he met the Nemean Lion?"

"Please don't go on —" said Hera faintly, but Tethys was caught up in the excitement of the story. "It was the first of the Ten Labours. Hera had arranged them, as you know. By then Heracles had grown into a tall, proud and handsome man, famous throughout the world for his strength and skill in battle."

"Taking after his father," said Zeus, with a smug smile.

"Yes," said Tethys. "Uncontrollable. No mortal man could defeat him, except his own self. And in a fit of mad temper, that's what happened. He misused his strength, destroying those dearest to him."

All the gods were looking at Hera, who had gone very pale.

"It's true Hera helped to cause it," said Tethys quietly. "But it was a weakness in Heracles's nature. A true hero must be strong inside as well as out. That is what his punishment — the Labours — taught him. Although that man-eating lion certainly tested his physical strength too!"

"It must have!" said Hermes, gaping at the gigantic beast that now spun into view. "No wonder the weapons we gave him weren't much use!"

Tethys laughed. "At least they made him feel some gods were on his side. But the Nemean Lion was the son of the monstrous ten-headed Typhon. Its skin was thick as dragon's scales. Apollo's arrows bounced off, blunted, and your sword, Hermes, bent like butter. As the lion leapt, razor-clawed, towards him, Heracles uprooted an olive tree, and smashed it into the creature's jaws. It stopped, stunned, then slunk into its lair. Without hesitation, Heracles followed it in there, and in that narrow space wrestled for his life. One finger bitten to the bone, one arm around the lion's throat, he used his weight to press it down and broke its neck."

"Original pankration," Zeus explained. But no one was listening. Everyone, including Hera, was looking at Tethys, who'd paused, spinning-wheel slowing to a stop.

"Go on!" they cried. "That's it," said Tethys. "Except that ever since he's worn the lion's skin. Clasped like a cloak with its claws."

"But the other Labours? That was only the first."

"I can't tell them *all*!" said Tethys. "It would take days! Particularly since crafty King Eurystheus insisted on twelve instead of ten. He set the tasks, although they were Hera's idea. Poor Heracles had to swallow his pride and do whatever he was told, with that cowardly king crowing over him. But then when Heracles kept coming back victorious, the king started crying! He was terrified. Especially when Heracles carried in the creatures he had captured! The Boar! The Bull! Worst of all . . . the Dog, Cerberus."

"That was the last Labour Eurystheus set. 'Bring back the Dog from the Land of the Dead.'

Athena led him to the world below, but Heracles had to enter alone, crossing the icy River Styx to the place of no return. Down in the dark the gates were barred, pale ghosts whispered his name. But he rattled the locks of the palace doors and at last Queen Persephone came. He warmed her with words of the bright world above and news of her mother Demeter. And she begged King Hades to let his hound go, so at last he agreed, to please her. But Cerberus had to be caught by hand, and carried away without collar or chains. If a weapon touched him at all he would be freed again.

Then the Dog was loosed, and his red eyes glowed as he hurled himself at Heracles. Three heads from one neck, three slathering mouths, three savage sets of teeth. But Heracles ducked and then reached up to choke his throat from underneath. When the animal coughed, he took him by the scruff, and shook until he gave in. Now Cerberus knew who was master, he lay across Heracles's shoulders, and didn't move a muscle until they came to Eurystheus."

"And then he only lifted one head!" said Hermes. "I couldn't believe my eyes. But when King Eurystheus saw them he was so afraid, he dived inside a pithos jar and wouldn't come out again!"

"No wonder he was scared!" said Athena. "Even I was surprised to see Heracles alive after that death-defying test!"

"But it wasn't the most difficult," said Tethys. "Not for Heracles. The hardest was cleaning stables for Augeas, King of Elis. Dealing with dung and filth and flies was no work for a hero! Bad enough to have to humble himself and serve his enemy Eurystheus. But for the son of Zeus to sweep out cow-sheds! When I saw him bend his back to that Labour – even if he did harness help from the river – I knew he had learned a true hero's power to endure. He had earned his immortality.

So that is why, when the Labours ended, and he was freed, when the battles were done, and the kingdom was won, Heracles returned to Elis. To that same cattle-trampled ground. The very place you see below you now. Look!"

Her wheel stilled, Tethys turned away, and pointed to the tele-viewer.

The Games had finished while she'd talked. The sun was setting on the stadium. "Down there," she said, "he measured out, heel to toe, six hundred of his massive feet. That set the course, and length of race mankind still run today. Then, the Altis made, he offered you his sacrifice. Gave thanks to Zeus for his success. And so began the Olympic Games."

"I remember," said Zeus, quietly. "I watched him race his chariot. And throw both discus and javelin. Then he picked up his great bow. All alone. What man could ever match him?"

"Then he looked up," Apollo cried, "and challenged us! I can't resist an archery contest!"

"Nor the stade race!" said Hermes. "We all leapt down for that!"

"Despite your wings, you didn't win!" Ares reminded him.

"But man and gods – we had such sport that day! Though only Zeus would wrestle Heracles."

"And drew," said Zeus. "I couldn't win outright. He held me in his famous ladder-grip."

"Which reminds me," said Apollo. "The pankration match, today. It's the great Polydamas. You know, the one who modelled himself on Heracles. He even managed to strangle a lion! I hope we haven't missed him."

"You haven't," said Tethys, laughing, "but there'll be no fight. His opponent was so afraid he ran away last night!"

41

**IT WAS THE FIFTH AND FINAL DAY – A TIME OF PRIZES AND PARADES.** In front of the statue of Zeus, the winners exchanged their woollen ribbon tokens for a victor's olive wreath, cut from the sacred 'tree of crowns'. Then they marched around the grove, led by Leonidas of Rhodes. For the third time running the whole Olympiad would be named after him. The praise-song especially composed to accompany his triumphant circuit was drowned by the excitement of the crowds. But the thin high flute could just be heard, setting feet tapping in delight.

Already fired up by yesterday's memories, most of the gods had slipped into human shape to join the joyous jostling of the Mortals down below.

Only Hera was still sitting by the tele-viewer, looking rather small on Zeus's great throne. She didn't notice Tethys coming up behind her until she felt herself caught up in her old nurse's arms, carried as if she was a child again. Sinking into softness, she closed her eyes.

When she opened them, she was surrounded by graceful columns of oak. On each one was a picture of a woman athlete – the winners of the Heraea Games. She was in her Temple, in the Altis. But today it was filled with Olympic athletes, waiting to go into the inner chamber, to honour her and give thanks for success. "They cannot see or hear you," said Tethys, pushing past, "except in their hearts."

In front of them now were two great statues. One showed Hera, seated on a throne. The other was Zeus, standing beside her. And between them was the beautiful bronze Disc of Iphitos, inscribed with the Olympic Truce.

"You know," Tethys said, "after Heracles and Pelops, the Olympiads continued in Elis for years. But eventually people forgot, and the Games stopped. Then times changed; a dark age came. The Kings of Greece grew greedy and quarrelsome. Cities were split by civil war, neighbours cheated each other, husbands and wives fought tooth and nail. Fertile land grew thin and poor, hunger howled and sickness spread.

Until at last King Iphitos went to the Delphic Oracle to ask how he could help his people. In that place of power, where Apollo slew the Python, by the stone at the earth's centre, he heard the Sybil speak:

'King Iphitos of Elis must hold the Games again. Throughout their duration a Sacred Truce must reign.'

And so it was that peace spread across Greece. Men came together to contest their strength in sport instead of war. And for the time it takes for all to travel to this sacred place, there must be no hostility among us."

"Oh Hera!" cried Tethys, smiling at her fondly, "the disc of Truce is housed in your Temple! Remember you are the Immortal Queen. Forget your silly squabbles, and show us how to be!"

All that night, the whole of Olympia rang with splendid banquet song. Spectators, sponsors, judges, trainers, athletes and all were celebrating wildly.

And up above on Mount Olympus the gods were feasting too. This time there were scents to suit all tastes. Heavenly Hera and her husband Zeus sat side by side in the great stone throne, sharing delicacies and some private joke.

Now the Games were over, the tele-viewer was blank, but Tethys and the three Fates stood round it, staring down.

"What do you see, Tethys?" asked Zeus.

"Only the Future," she said with a sigh. "Further ahead than you can even dream."

"Are the Mortals still holding Olympic Games?"

"Yes," said Tethys. "But they've changed. I see men and women athletes taking turns in the same stadium, watched by anyone who cares to go and see. Or even by those who are far far away! Mortals will have tele-viewers too, one day."

The Shining One just shook his head. It was Hera who answered for him. "Tethys," she said, "we all love to hear your stories. Because we know they really happened, too. But this Future sounds like a Mortal's fairy tale. Only children could believe it is true!"

# A NOTE FROM THE AUTHOR

This book began, as well as ended, at the British Museum. In 2010 they held a special 'Ancient Olympics Sleepover' and I was storyteller. I knew I must mention most of the Greek gods, in whose honour the Games were held. I'd also have to talk about all the heroes, heroines and legends associated with specific sports.

But I was afraid that introducing so many names and personalities could be confusing for a family audience. I needed a link or character to make everything connect easily. Then I met 'Tethys'.

One of the first Titans, she was there at the very beginning. Auntie to the elder gods, and related to almost everybody else through her thousands of watery children, her name reveals her nature. 'Tethys' means 'nanny': both nurse and grandmother.

Nannies know all about everyone, and will soon make sure that you do too. And they are essential peacemakers in any fractious family gathering, particularly immortal ones. Tethys must have been there, or everything would have ended in tears!

Despite her importance, there are scarcely any tales told about her. Maybe she was just too good at telling other peoples' stories. Certainly once she took on mine, they simply flowed.

But even in Tethys's capable hands, there were lots of lovely little tributaries of legend and Olympic lore we could not follow up. So for those who want to know if discus-throwing began at Troy, and that pole-vaulting high jump was invented to escape from the Calydonian Boar, or just to find out more about the gods and heroic characters in this book, here are a few of my main sources:

Judith Swaddling, *The Ancient Olympic Games* (British Museum Press, 1980, updated 2011)
Richard Woff, *The Ancient Greek Olympics* (British Museum Press, 1999)
Robert Graves, *The Greek Myths* (Penguin, 1991)
Any good encyclopedia of Classic myths – the one I read most avidly as a child (spurred on by being named Helen) was Bulfinch's *Mythology* (1855–63; Modern Library, 1998)

Thanks also to my father for taking me to Troy, my mother for showing me the British Museum, Sally Pomme Clayton and June Peters for sharing stories, Naomi Waters and Felicity Maunder for excellent editing, and Rick for everything.

Helen East, www.eastorywilsound.co.uk

# A NOTE FROM THE ILLUSTRATOR

I also began work on this book by going to the British Museum. I was looking for general inspiration and to get the right atmosphere for my illustrations. It was the pictures on the Greek and Roman pottery that I loved best. Very old, some only fragments or small bits, but each of them was telling a story. Sometimes there was writing too, above or below, giving the names of the characters. Perfect! I wonder if you can guess which ones inspired me most?

Merdokht Amini, www.myart2c.com

To learn more about objects in the British Museum, visit www.britishmuseum.org